To Julie—lover of museums and captain of our Explorers

With love and thanks to Jamal and Meka Tull

A FEIWEL AND FRIENDS BOOK
An imprint of Macmillan Publishing Group, LLC
120 Broadway, New York, NY 10271

EXPLORERS. Copyright © 2019 by Matthew Cordell. All rights reserved.
Printed in China by RR Donnelley Asia Printing Solutions Ltd., Dongguan City, Guangdong Province.

Our books may be purchased in bulk for promotional, educational, or business use.
Please contact your local bookseller or the Macmillan Corporate and Premium
Sales Department at (800) 221-7945 ext. 5442 or by email at MacmillanSpecialMarkets@macmillan.com.

Library of Congress Control Number: 2019931336

ISBN 978-1-250-17496-3

Book design by Sophie Erb
Feiwel and Friends logo designed by Filomena Tuosto

First edition, 2019

The artwork was created with pen and ink with watercolor.

1 3 5 7 9 10 8 6 4 2

mackids.com

Matthew Cordell

Feiwel and Friends | New York

KSSHHH H

snatch!!